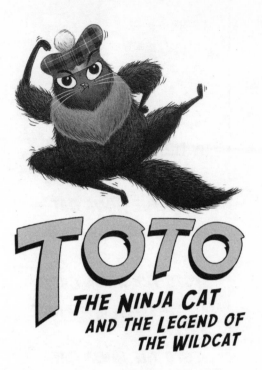

TOTO

THE NINJA CAT
AND THE LEGEND OF THE WILDCAT

  This book belongs to:

BY DERMOT O'LEARY

TOTO THE NINJA CAT
AND THE GREAT SNAKE ESCAPE

TOTO THE NINJA CAT
AND THE INCREDIBLE CHEESE HEIST

TOTO THE NINJA CAT
AND THE SUPERSTAR CATASTROPHE

TOTO THE NINJA CAT
AND THE MYSTERY JEWEL THIEF

TOTO THE NINJA CAT
AND THE LEGEND OF THE WILDCAT

TOTO
THE NINJA CAT
AND THE LEGEND OF
THE WILDCAT

DERMOT O'LEARY

ILLUSTRATED BY NICK EAST

h HODDER

HODDER CHILDREN'S BOOKS

First published in Great Britain in 2021 by Hodder & Stoughton
This edition published in 2022

3 5 7 9 10 8 6 4 2

A CIP catalogue record for this book
is available from the British Library.

ISBN 978 1 444 96168 3

Printed and bound in Great Britain by Clays Ltd, Elcograf S.p.A.
The paper and board used in this book are made from wood from
responsible sources

MIX
Paper from
responsible sources
FSC® C104740

Hodder Children's Books
An imprint of Hachette Children's Group
Part of Hodder & Stoughton Limited
Carmelite House
50 Victoria Embankment
London EC4Y 0DZ
An Hachette UK Company
www.hachette.co.uk
www.hachettechildrens.co.uk

TO KASPER.

THANKS FOR THE LAUGHS, THE INSPIRATION,
THE SMILES AND FOR BEING A CAPTIVE AUDIENCE.

SOCKS AND TOTO DO RESPECTFULLY ASK IF YOU
WOULDN'T MIND BEING A LITTLE LESS 'GRABBY'.

X

PROLOGUE

The mist was still heavy on the water when the unlikely pair of old friends emerged from the bushes at the top of the beach and made their way down to the water's edge to collect their quarry.

The rat and stoat were poachers. They had hidden in the undergrowth for the last few hours, ever watchful for the prying eyes of the human gamekeeper and his terrifying, bloodthirsty scent hound. The dog, Herbert, and the gamekeeper, Colin, had fearsome reputations for chasing down trespassers on their land (in spite of their not-so-scary names!). So any animal out in the cold spring dawn had better keep their wits about them, or risk being torn to shreds.

Slowly, the pair stretched out their tired limbs – they were frozen stiff and eager to get back to the warmth of their fires. Both the old pals had been poachers for as long as they could remember, though they didn't like the term being used in a negative way. As far as they and most animals were concerned, this was as much their land as any human's. Their fathers and mothers and grandparents before them had all taken the prized salmon and trout from the shores of the loch. Herbert and Colin weren't about to stop them now.

ARCHIE MACTABB, the smaller of the two, was a thin wiry stoat with brown fur and a brilliant-white underbelly. He was famed across the whole of the Scottish wilds for his quick thinking and ability to wriggle his way in and out of the tiniest cracks and burrows in the ground. He was the first to move from their hiding place, his small feet padding quickly across the smooth beach to the shoreline, where he began to scratch around in the sand to uncover a rope tied to an iron peg. He shook the sand from the rope and began to haul in their net from the chilly water as fast as he could.

'What on earth is your hurry, Archie?' His friend smiled as he ambled down to the water's edge. **SANDY CAMPBELL** was an impressive-looking rat. Dressed in a waxed jacket and flat cap he was every inch the Scottish gentleman. He was loved and admired by most of the wild animals in

Scotland and widely regarded as the **_KING OF THE POACHERS._**

'Well, for one thing I'm stone-cold and hungry, and I'd quite like to get back to my warm farmhouse. Plus, if we don't haul in these fish and get them to our customers by eight o'clock there'll be hell to pay. So do me a favour and come and give me a hand. Less chat, more do!'

'OK, OK, don't get your fur in a tangle. I'm coming,' the rat replied cheerfully.

The haul was good; a bounty of trout and crayfish meant that the poachers could look forward to a well-earned rest.

'We'll get these loaded on to the cart, three drop-offs and a bag of crayfish for each of us and we're home dry,' said Sandy as he stopped to mop his brow with a hanky. 'Odd that the mist is still on the water. You'd have thought it would have gone by this time.'

As Sandy glanced at his friend for a response, he recognised the look of sheer terror in the small stoat's eyes and knew immediately what it meant. He turned to see the **ENORMOUS HOUND** and its owner emerging from a nearby bush. The poachers weren't the only ones who had been watching and waiting – they'd been beaten at their own game and now they'd pay the price.

'This is the last time you two will get the better of me,' Herbert snarled, his enormous razor-sharp fangs covered in drool. Colin leered down at them with an evil grin on his face.

'I'm sorry, Archie,' Sandy gulped. 'Looks like we'll not be making it home this time.'

The mist was now so thick he could barely see his paw in front of his face, but it didn't matter; from this distance there could be no escape. For the briefest of moments Sandy thought he heard a **DISTANT HOWL,** probably just some old cat on the way home. He shut his eyes and waited for the end ... and waited, and once again ... waited. Nothing. He dared to open one eye for a peek, and almost had to close it again in shock: Colin was running away clutching his arm in pain and Herbert was rolling around in agony, yelping, scratch marks on his face.

He turned bewildered to his partner. 'Well, that was a surprise. I didn't know you had it in you!' But his friend ignored him, staring in shock at a rock behind the rat. Sandy turned and looked up to see the mist part and there, standing on top of the outcrop on its hind legs, was an **ENORMOUS, MAJESTIC CAT.** To the untrained eye it looked like a big domestic tabby, but both Sandy and Archie knew exactly who it was and they could barely believe their eyes.

The cat stood motionless for a second or two, seemingly studying the pair, then a small but definite smile crossed its face. It gave the tiniest of nods to Sandy and Archie and then, with a leap, it was gone. As the figure vanished, so too did the mist that surrounded the loch.

Herbert had now got to his paws and went howling off after his human as Sandy helped his friend up.

'Who'd have thought it,' Archie said in awe. 'After all these years.'

Sandy nodded, speechless. He was just as amazed, but there was something else on his mind ... He'd have to get word to his friends in London: **THE LEGENDARY WILDCAT WAS BACK.**

CHAPTER 1

'Of course I can do it. It's a piece of cake, especially for a fully fledged ninja deputy!'

Everyone in the milk bar roared with laughter and encouragement. Toto the Ninja Cat sat at the end of the table, her head in her paws, trying not to laugh and praying her dear friend and two brothers didn't do anything too stupid.

The cats were celebrating, and with good reason. They had recently foiled the evil King Roderick the Spotlessly Clean's dastardly plan to steal the animal Crown Jewels, frame Toto's boss Larry, raise an army of rats and pretty much destroy everything on earth (it was a *weird* plan). And they had done such a good job that Larry had bestowed the title of **DEPUTY NINJA CAT** on Toto's brothers Silver and Socks and their dear friend Catface (the most popular cat-rat in London town). While this was a huge honour, Larry was at **GREAT PAINS** to point out: 'It certainly **does not** mean you are actual ninjas.'

For one thing, none of them had the patience to get through the training, which took *ages*. Plus, although they were all brave (and for that alone, Toto was proud of all three of them), none were terribly gifted in the fighting department. Silver wasn't bad but, in his own words, the training 'got in the way of good eating time'. Socks was spirited but too tiny to fight off anyone with big muscles. Catface had fenced as a young rat, and had picked up the odd move from Toto, but, as he readily admitted, he was 'mostly hopeless at that sort of thing'.

But being a deputy ninja came with a badge and an allowance of twenty-five litres of Jersey milk and five hampers of cheese a year ... and that was not to be sniffed at. So after the ceremony the team had decided to celebrate at **THE LEGENDARY MILK BAR THE SOUR SAUCER,** under Blackfriars Bridge on the banks of the River Thames.

The last time the cats had been here the atmosphere had been very different: the whole bar had been full of cut-throats and smugglers intent on making them walk the famous plank that jutted out over the cold waters of the river below. Luckily, thanks to Toto, that gang was behind bars now, and while the clientele was still on the salty side (mostly made up of ships' dogs, rats and cats) it was a lot safer to drink in. So Catface, Silver and Socks had been making the most of their Jersey milk allowance and were now keen to take on the challenge of the plank ... which brings us back to why Toto had her head in her paws ...

'A piece of cake! I'll wager with any one of you fine ladies or gents that I, Catface, Alexandre Rattinoff the Thirty-third, and my two fellow deputies can leap from the plank, **SOMERSAULT IN THE AIR** and land perfectly on that lovely boat moored below without getting even one strand of our fur wet. What say you all to my bet ... a litre of your best milk? Henry! Set them up, we'll be back in a jiffy.'

Henry, the landlord of The Sour Saucer, who was an enormous, gruff, but well-meaning Maine Coon, rolled his eyes and went back to drying glasses.

'Come on then, chaps, away we go.' Catface ushered his friends towards the plank. They didn't look entirely convinced this was a good idea.

'Catface, are you sure about this? It's dark and – *MAMMA MIA!* – an awfully long way down,' Silver kind-of-protested.

'Too right, bro, and I'm not exactly the world's best swimmer,' said Socks.

'Oh, stuff and nonsense,' replied Catface. 'You won't even get your paws wet. Think of all the tips you've picked up from your sister down the years. Now, come, gentlemen.'

The rat turned once more to the patrons of the bar, who were all now enthralled at what might happen. 'My friends, witness the awesome skill, bravery and power of the deputy ninjas. We shall rejoin you anon!'

At this the rat **LEAPT INTO THE DARK VOID,** followed reluctantly by Silver and Socks. The whole of the bar crowded around the windows to watch. Toto raced to a window herself, and even though she was almost totally blind, she could just about make out the shadows of shapes hurtling through the night air.

Despite Catface's false bravado, all three managed to perform some pretty impressive somersaults as he was yelling, 'See, what did I tell you!'

Toto couldn't help but feel a little proud ... until they crashed through the deck of the beautiful little yacht one by one, going straight through the hull and splitting it in two. The trio disappeared under the water for a second but, thankfully, surfaced quickly and swam to the safety of the nearby jetty.

THE BOAT WASN'T SO LUCKY.

Toto and everyone else rushed down to the jetty in time to see the last tip of the boat's bow disappear with a hiss into the dark river below. All eyes descended on Catface, Silver and Socks.

'Oh blast, that bit wasn't supposed to happen. But you have to admit, the somersaults were first class, weren't they?' Catface said sheepishly. 'I say, does anyone know who owns the yacht? I'll happily pay for a new one. I'm sure they'll understand. After all, it was an accident.'

'Toto, do you have any idea who owns that boat?' Henry the landlord said with a wince.

'No, why?' replied the ninja, intrigued.

The huge cat gave Toto a commiserating pat on the shoulder. 'Let's just say, it might not be that easy to talk your way out of, even for Catfa—'

'MY PRIDE AND JOY, *THE LEAPING LANGOUSTINE*! I ONLY MOORED HER HERE TWO HOURS AGO TO GO TO THE BALLET! WHO DID THIS? I'LL STRING THEM UP BY THEIR TAILS!'

All eyes turned to the old ginger cat with a massive moustache who was marching down the gangway. On a list of 'whose boat not to accidentally sink', he pretty much came top. It was the pompous animal Home Secretary Sir Wigbert Fluffypaws the Third, who had recently – and incorrectly – accused Larry of stealing the Crown Jewels and tried to use it as an excuse to get rid of the Ninja Cats. Luckily, they had been able to prove him wrong and make him look like the old

GRRRRR

windbag he was – and they'd been sworn enemies ever since. Annoyingly, this time he was in the right!

'Who, I say? Just give me a name!' he screamed. *THE CROWD PARTED TO LEAVE TOTO AND THE SOAKING-WET CATFACE, SOCKS AND SILVER TO FACE THE MUSIC.*

'Oh boy,' Silver groaned. 'No litter tray on earth is deep enough for the cat poo we're in right now.'

'I might have known the ninja clot and her idiot deputies would be responsible. Well, you'll be for the chop now – none of your fancy moves or your sassy words or your high-up friends are going to save you lot this time. Revenge will be mine and it will be so, so sweet! Larry's office tomorrow,

6 a.m. sharp,' he bellowed, then turned and stomped back up the gangway followed by his wife, Lady Fluffypaws, who smiled apologetically at the gang.

'I'm sure you didn't mean it, dears, but Wigbert does have quite the temper. By the way, don't tell anyone, but I hated that yacht, so thank you!' she whispered.

'Well, she seems nice!' said Catface as the crowd dispersed, leaving the four friends on the jetty.

'Sorry, sis,' meowed Socks. 'You'll get in all sorts of trouble for this.'

'No,' interjected Catface as he wrung out his coat. 'I'm the fool here. I got carried away and my new ninja authority went to my head. I'll take full responsibility.'

'It WAS a really, really stupid thing to do,' replied Toto, 'but I appreciate it.'

'Tell you what though, sis,' said Silver with a smile. 'You must be doing something right with your teaching – our somersaults were on point!'

CHAPTER 2

If the muffled shouting coming from Larry's office was anything to go by, the poor Ninja Cat boss was getting it in the neck from the Home Secretary. They couldn't make out every single word, although **IDIOT, FOOLS** and **NINCOMPOOP** featured heavily. Fluffypaws wasn't holding back and the cats could tell he was enjoying every minute.

The door swung open to reveal an angry but triumphant Sir Fluffypaws. He stood for a moment looking down at Toto and her gang. 'You should count yourselves lucky. If I had my way, you'd all be exiled to Van Felines land, like we did with ne'er-do-wells back in the old days. Perkins!' he screamed to a tiny white Singapura cat in a black suit who looked like he was quite terrified of Fluffypaws. 'Call Claridge's, tell them to book my usual table for lunch. I've worked up quite the appetite and I fancy three courses. *REVENGE, JUSTICE AND JUST DESERTS FOR PUDDING!* Pah! I say, that was rather good, wasn't it? Sally forth!'

He brushed everyone in the corridor aside and stormed out of the building, with poor

Perkins following on behind.

'In here. Now.'

The cats looked up to see Larry shaking his head at them. They sheepishly shuffled into his office and closed the door behind them.

'Oh no, he's not angry, he's disappointed ... that's the worst,' Silver whispered to Toto, who was feeling more and more like she'd badly let Larry down. It might not have been **EXACTLY** her fault, but it **WAS** her responsibility. As the only fully fledged Ninja Cat it was down to her to uphold the good name of the order.

'What on earth were you thinking? Actually, don't answer that; you weren't. Do you have any idea of the grief this has caused me? Since the retrieval of the Crown Jewels, Fluffypaws' name has been a laughing stock, which meant the one enemy we had in the animal government had been sidelined. He has even just been demoted to **MINISTER FOR HORSE MANURE,** and trust me, that's a job no one wants.'

Silver and Socks looked at each other and suppressed a laugh.

'Exactly, it should be hilarious!' continued Larry. 'But when you lot all decided to jump out of that window and destroy his boat you gave him ammunition to come after the Ninja Cats again!'

'Sorry, boss,' they answered in unison.

'He wanted to throw the book at you: strip you of your deputy status and even suspend Toto!' The little ninja swallowed hard. To be suspended would be the worst – she'd prefer to resign than bring shame and embarrassment on the order. Luckily Larry's tone softened. 'The PM wouldn't hear of it, given all the work you've been doing up to now bu—'

'Huzzah, all's well that ends well!' cried Catface, and went to help himself to a drink at Larry's milk cabinet.

'Not so fast! That doesn't mean you're out of the woods,' the ninja boss said reproachfully. 'Have any of you heard of **GLENVIEW CORRECTIONAL CAMP?**'

Socks gulped.

'I'm taking it that's not a good gulp,' Silver whispered, and his little brother shook his head.

'Quite right, young Socks,' Larry continued. 'Glenview is a beautiful camp in the wilds of Scotland. Sadly for you four, that's the only thing lovely about it. It's been going for fifty years now, with incredible results. Any animal who's been a bit naughty – you know the kind of thing: **_BITEY SHEEPDOGS, SCRATCHY CATS, PARROTS WHO USE NAUGHTY WORDS_** – gets sent there and after some ... err, let's say *correctional activities*, they come out the other side a model animal. And you four are off there for a week, taking the train from Euston Station first thing tomorrow morning.'

Socks and Silver let out a groan, but Catface looked quite chipper about the news.

'Don't groan at me,' their boss chuckled, clearly enjoying their discomfort. 'This is the best I could do. Count yourselves lucky old Fluffypaws isn't better connected!'

The cats headed for the door, and Larry went back to studying papers on his desk before adding, 'Did he really blow a gasket when you sank the boat?'

'He was furious.' Catface grinned.

'Terrible news,' said Larry, suppressing a smile. 'Toto, can you stay behind for a word?'

The little ninja's heart dropped. This was it; she was in for it now. She shut the door behind the others.

'BOSS, I AM SO SORRY. I should have done something, but everything happened so quickly. Before I knew it, they'd jumped out of The Sour Saucer and to be fair, you should have seen the somersaults – they were really something else ...' she trailed off. Larry wasn't listening and was more engrossed in a map of Scotland on his wall. 'Boss?'

'What?' Larry looked round, distracted. 'Oh, don't worry about that. I don't blame you at all, and a week away from home comforts will do that lot no harm whatsoever. I'm just sorry I have to ask you to go as well, but for an entirely different reason. Please, sit down.'

He poured them both a glass of creamy milk before continuing. 'Toto, what do you know about the legend of "Felis of Grampia and the Wildcats of Scotland"?'

'Absolutely nothing,' answered the little ninja. 'Should I?'

'No, I'm not surprised; not many animals outside of Scotland do. There was a time when the wildcat clans ruled all the animals of Scotland, inspiring loyalty and fear in equal measure. *THEY WERE THE MIGHTIEST WARRIORS IN THE WORLD AND JUST AS EXALTED AS US NINJAS.* They were seen as fair and just to most animals and were good rulers, and they were legendary fighters – no army could beat them.'

Toto was fascinated; they seemed like her kind of cats.

'What happened to them?' she asked.

'Sadly, mankind did.' Larry sighed. 'They were hunted, seen as pests and a danger to livestock. The last few were thought to have disappeared a couple of hundred years ago.'

'Sorry, I don't quite follow. What has this got to do with me going to Scotland?'

Larry refilled Toto's glass and sat at the table opposite her.

'Local legend has it that a few wildcats still remain, the descendants of the great clan chiefs – living nomadic lives wandering the Highlands – and that one day they will rise up, march on Edinburgh and claim their rightful place as the last cat kings of Scotland.'

'But if it's just a legend, then what's the problem?'

'Up until last week, it felt as far-fetched as Nessie.'

'Excuse me?'

'Really? You don't know about the **LOCH NESS MONSTER?** They taught you nothing in that Italian ninja school. Never mind. Last week my contact up there thinks he may have spotted Felis.'

'Thinks?'

'Well, he's a superstitious old so-and-so. He probably just saw a large domestic cat; there are loads of sightings every year that come to nothing. Mostly domestic cats on their holidays who love the legend and are into the whole wildcat re-enactment scene. Quite odd if you ask me. But I feel duty-bound to investigate so when your brothers sank Fluffypaws' yacht it gave me the perfect opportunity to send you there to find out more.'

'I'm to travel up with the boys tomorrow?'

'Tickets and papers right here,' said Larry, opening his drawer. 'There are a couple of things I need you to know. One: you are undercover. The last thing we need is the animal press getting hold of this and causing a panic. Which brings me on to my next point—'

'**NO NINJA MOVES?**' guessed Toto with a sigh.

'No ninja moves. Sorry, Toto, but if anyone at the camp guesses who you are, we'll be rumbled. So I've decided you should use a secret identity for the week.' He passed over the tickets and a Braille ID card.

Toto moved her paws over the Braille. 'Tiddles Braithwaite hardly sounds like the name of a naughty cat!'

'Oh, you'd be surprised.' Larry grinned. 'Read on.'

'One female owner, Gladys Braithwaite, aged eighty-two, of 14 Winterbottom Avenue, Croydon. Sentenced to a week at Glenview Correctional Camp for –' Toto looked up at Larry ' – attempting to eat the pet budgie Petula? Larry, **EVERYONE HATES BUDGIE-KILLERS;** they are the lowest of the low!'

'That's right. But everyone is scared of them too, so no one will mess with you. It's the perfect cover. Oh, I forgot, you'll be needing this.' He threw **A YELLOW WOOL COAT, A HAT AND A PAIR OF GLASSES TO TOTO.** 'Lovely, no one will recognise you.'

'It will make me look like an old lady!'

'Exactly!' he exclaimed. 'Now, get in character, keep an eye on those trouble-making boys and report back to me if you find anything – which I'm sure you won't.'

Toto left feeling pretty relaxed about the week ahead, even with a silly outfit to wear. Since the chances of the legend being real were pretty much non-existent, all she had to do was observe and try to keep her brothers and Catface out of trouble.

IF ONLY IT WAS GOING TO BE THAT EASY ...

CHAPTER 3

It was a cold and miserable morning – the kind where the damp air chills you to the bone – as the gang congregated at Euston Station ready for their journey to Scotland. The cats had been able to get away for the week, as their human mamma and papa had just had a baby, so were a bit distracted. While the cats were still very much doted on, the new arrival was in Silver's words a little 'grabby'. So, in many ways the week away couldn't have come at a better time.

The gang had packed light with just small knapsacks, apart from Catface, of course. The stylish cat-rat was dressed in a green tweed blazer and a blue-and-green-tartan kilt, with a sporran, long socks and brogues, all topped off with a traditional Balmoral bonnet. And he had a huge trunk in tow.

'I have to admit, I am quite looking forward to this: the bracing clean air in our lungs, a spot of fishing on the loch, cosy peat fires in the evening. I might even call in on my cousin. I think I'll have to write to old Fluffypaws and thank him!' Catface said with a chuckle.

'Catface mate, where do you think we're going?' Socks asked, looking baffled. 'What exactly do you think Glenview is?'

'And what is that?' Silver pointed to the small pouch hanging from Catface's hips.

'That, my young Italian friend, is a sporran – sort of like a pocket for a kilt. I am dressed in my old family tartan; my mother's side of the family is Scottish. And I'm well aware of where we are going: a charming place called Glenview ... which I assume is some kind of animal finishing school? I attended one in Switzerland many years ago, so I imagine we'll be learning deportment, etiquette and so on. Should be a breeze.'

Socks put his paw to his head and let out a groan. 'Catface, *IT'S A CORRECTIONAL*

CAMP RUN BY THE MILITARY. Loads of my mates from Battersea have been sent up there – it's got a terrible reputation. This week is going to be brutal!'

'Well, we'll see about that! I say, my dear man, can you help me with my luggage and direct me to the restaurant car?' Catface called over to a stern-looking bulldog dressed in regimental khakis and a peaked cap worn low over his eyes, who was studying a clipboard and was obviously in a position of authority.

He slowly looked Catface up and down and smiled, then said in a heavy Scottish accent, **'WHY, OF COURSE, YOUR MAJESTY, FOLLOW ME. OOH, ALLOW ME TO TAKE YOUR CASE, IT LOOKS AWFULLY HEAVY.'**

Catface followed on behind. 'See,' he beamed at his friends. 'A little bit of politeness goes a long wa—'

He was interrupted by the bulldog grabbing the lapel of his blazer and hauling him towards the train. 'Name?' he barked.

'Err, FatCace, I mean, Rattinoff ... the Thirty-third ... Alexandre,' he spluttered.

The bulldog looked down at his list and ticked off Catface's name. 'You three boys are the jokers who sank the Right Honourable Sir Fluffypaws' boat. Got ourselves some troublemakers, have we?'

'I wouldn't quite say that. It was a rather terrible accide—'

'Silence!' the bulldog screamed at Catface. 'You speak only when you are spoken to!'

'Strictly speaking, you *were* speaking to us ... Oh never mind,' Catface muttered under his breath.

'My name is Sergeant Major Gordon. For this next miserable week of your lives you will address me as Sergeant. I am here to somehow turn this train of unruly, useless **GOOD-FOR-NOTHINGS** into something approximating a lean, disciplined outfit, capable of taking orders. I'm going to be taking personal interest in making sure you three pass with flying colours and return to London as obedient, dutiful animals. Make no mistake, this will be the **TOUGHEST WEEK** of your lives. Now, get on board and, in answer to your question, the dining car is at the back of the train. They serve porridge,

porridge and more porridge, which is all you'll be eating this whole long, painful week. That's how an army wins a battle ... **PORRIDGE!!!!**' he bellowed.

He turned to go, but caught sight of Toto in her bright-yellow outfit.

'Name?' he barked.

'Braithwaite. Tiddles Braithwaite,' she answered quickly.

He checked his clipboard. 'Oh, our resident budgie-hater. I'll be keeping my eye on you; one of my best friends is a budgie called Alan. You've got a VERY hard week ahead of you,' he said in disgust, and turned on his heels to bark orders at some unfortunate rat porters who were loading the train.

'I say, do you think we've got the right train? I'm sure Larry has made a *TERRIBLE ERROR.* I wonder if it's too late to send him a woodpecker-gram?' sighed Catface just as a conductor cried 'All aboard!' and a whistle came from the huge lumbering locomotive.

'We're definitely in the right place,' Toto replied. 'And we've already got on the wrong side of the most important animal here ... which is great, if not unsurprising. Come on, let's get a seat while we can and TRY to keep our heads down.'

The cats managed to find a free compartment towards the back. It was a world away from the last time they'd travelled by rail, to the great animal music festival of Catstonbury. That train had had luxurious sleeping berths and a fancy dining car, whereas this one felt more like a prison. Luckily, Silver had smuggled some **CHEESE SANDWICHES** (mature Cheddar) from home, so they were all able to enjoy an early lunch before settling down to take in the view as the skies cleared and the city gave way to fields, long winding canals and green woods.

The peace was broken by a **LOUD CRASHING NOISE** coming down the carriage, then their door was slung open. A huge brown cat entered and it was clear his intentions weren't friendly.

'I've found one,' he called over his shoulder. 'There's four of them in here, but I'm sure they won't mind vacating.' He smiled menacingly. Three other cats appeared behind him. A blunt-nosed, well-built tabby, who was clearly the leader, barged his way in, followed by two smaller Burmese cats.

Socks slunk down in his seat and whispered to Silver, 'I know him. He's Harry and they're called the **MEOWSIDERS** – a horrible gang who bully and terrorise animals around South London. My gang, the Battersea Bruisers, has clashed with them before. They aren't to be messed with. I'm not surprised they're on the train.'

'Well well, if it isn't tiny Socksie,' Harry sneered as he clocked the little cat. 'And who are this lot – your new family? We heard you left Battersea. Think you're too good to be hanging out with the likes of us any more? Well, we'll happily teach you a lesson, won't we, guys?' The cats all laughed mockingly.

'Nice to see you too, Harry. You been sent up here for running that hamster wheel racket again? Must feel very big stealing from those poor little fluffy fellas,' retorted Socks bravely.

'Serves them right, hibernating all the time. If they ain't awake, they won't know what we've half-inched,' he cackled.

'Speaking of which, my poor legs are getting very tired so perhaps you and your friends could kindly *GET OUT!*'

This was agony for Toto. She hated bullies above all else. But she couldn't blow her cover; it would ruin the whole mission before it had even begun. It was with immense pride but also concern that she felt Silver stand up to confront Harry. 'Listen, you can see this carriage is taken. We don't want any trouble, but don't make us get angry,' he said, managing to keep his voice steady.

'Oh really, we wouldn't like it if you were angry? I'm quaking in my boots.'

'Simply petrified,' one of the Burmese cats added with a smirk.

'You have been warned,' replied Silver

and, surprising everyone, not least Toto, he launched himself at the leader of the gang. His hind legs connected with the bigger cat and sent him *FLYING AGAINST THE WALL.*

Everyone was stunned. Toto was impressed by her brother's technique, but she was also fearful of what was coming. A second later, the other three Meowsiders piled on to Silver, picked him up and threw him down the corridor of the train, where he landed in a painful heap.

Harry had dusted himself off and grabbed Catface and Socks by the scruffs of their necks. 'And you lot can follow him if you know what's good for you.'

'Err, Ms, um, Tiddles?' Catface stammered, but the little ninja shook her head.

THIS WAY
UP

'What are you lot staring at that old bat for? All of you GET OUT of our carriage. NOW.'

Toto led the way and went to the aid of her brother as the Meowsiders closed the door and roared with laughter again.

Toto pulled her brother to his feet, and with nowhere else to sit they made for the back of the train where they sat outside on the caboose. It had started to rain, so they huddled together and for a while said nothing.

'Well, so far we've made enemies with both our Sergeant Major and the most notorious gang in London. *I'D SAY IT'S ALL GOING RATHER WELL*, wouldn't you?' chuckled Catface.

'I didn't know you'd mastered the high kick,' Toto said, giving her brother a friendly lick.

'What can I say, sis? I learnt from the best!' Silver smiled, but winced a little in pain.

'The Sergeant Major wasn't wrong when he said we'd got a tough week ahead of us,' Socks said sheepishly.

'At least we have old budgie-hater here to help,' said Catface. 'Although I have to say, these missions aren't half easier when you're not undercover.'

CHAPTER 4

With the sound of the rain tapping on the roof of the train, and with the warmth of being all cuddled together, the cats eventually dropped off to sleep. By the time they awoke they had almost finished their journey into the wilds of Scotland. While Catface knew the country well, the rest of the cats were taken aback by its beauty. As the train snaked its way over a viaduct, the cats looked out on to a picturesque loch that stretched as far as the eye could see. On each side of the water, the mountains grew steep, turning into snow-lined peaks that looked to the cats as close to the stars as they could imagine.

'I've never seen such a sight,' Socks said, amazed.

'*Bellissimo*. I had no idea Britain was this beautiful,' sighed Silver as he explained the view to Toto.

Catface smiled. 'Quite something, isn't it? I'll never forget the first time I saw Scotland; my mother took me up to meet family as a little baby rat. Now, Glenview shouldn't be far, so let's get ready and keep our wits

about us. If these Meowsiders are anything to go by, I can't imagine we'll get the best reception.'

'Exactly,' Toto agreed. 'And please **REMEMBER THAT I'M UNDERCOVER,** so I can't help you if you get into any more trouble. Let's keep our heads down, get through the week and investigate these wildcat sightings. We'll be back safe and sound before you know it.'

Sure enough, as the long locomotive curved around the bend of the hill, the view opened up to reveal a huge glen in the distance, nestled in the shadow of a giant mountain. The train pulled into the station, the doors opened and the motley group of passengers stepped on to the platform.

The Meowsiders looked over at Toto and her friends and gave them a sarcastic wave. Elsewhere there were dogs, cats, foxes, ferrets, a couple of magpies and a pair of cold-looking bearded dragons. Some looked tough, like this wasn't their first time at Glenview. Others looked very scared, like they'd rather be anywhere else.

Sergeant Major Gordon appeared at the head of the platform and bellowed in a voice so loud that Toto and the cats could hear every word he said.

'Glenview is a ten-mile march. Fall into two lines and follow me. Anyone trying to escape will be dealt with swiftly and without mercy. Quiiiiick march!'

A platoon of uniformed and dangerous-looking Border terriers fell into line next to the new recruits and they all made their way into the countryside. A few miles in, as they passed through a pine forest, Toto became distracted by a pair of agitated ferrets in front of her.

'I can't take it, Michael, not this place again. I can't help nipping the odd finger or two, it's in my nature. But this place, those tasks, it's barbaric I tell you. Plus most of the animals here are as bad as the guards, I swear. I want no part of it; I'll go crazy.'

MP
TRAMP

'Don't be daft, Steven. We'll get out of here in a month or so. Just take it easy.' But the nervy ferret wasn't having any of it; he had spotted a small path to the left that led through the

67

forest and, glancing around for the Border terriers, whose attention was momentarily elsewhere, he darted for it. The bulldog at the front of the column seemed to have eyes in the back of his head and no sooner had Steven reached the cover of the bracken the Sergeant Major bellowed, 'Terriers! Red Alert!'

The platoon of Border terriers sprang into action and disappeared into the undergrowth to make chase, barking loudly. Nobody could see what happened, but the loud yelps made it clear that the poor unfortunate ferret hadn't made it far. Within minutes he was brought back, covered in bruises, and dumped at the feet of his concerned partner.

Sergeant Major Gordon looked over the

animals before him and boomed, 'Let this pathetic specimen be an example to the lot of you. You will serve your time, you will be rehabilitated and you will obey the rules of the camp. Anyone who refuses to do so ... Well, you see the penalty. Now, if no one else wishes to escape?' The crowd stayed silent. 'Excellent. FORWARD MARCH,' he yelled.

'I think this week might be a little harder than Larry led us to believe,' Silver whispered to his sister.

'It's OK, brother. If we stick together, we'll make it out of here just fine.'

But underneath, Toto was worried. The poor ferret had taken a beating, and knowing Catface and her two brothers, there was no way they would stay out of trouble. Plus there was something else the ferret had said that troubled her: 'Most of the animals here are as bad as the guards ...' It was an odd thing to say. Could the camp really be that bad?

A few miles later they finally made it through the forest and out into a valley banked by steep green hills. There ahead of them was Glenview. The camp was made up of lots of tented structures and in the centre was a huge parade ground, which was where the march finally ended.

'Line up, line up, stand to attention for the officers,' Sergeant Major Gordon barked fiercely as the tired column of animals came to a halt.

At the front of the parade ground was a large hut with a covered wooden porch. Standing to await the arrival of the column were two portly, imposing-looking animals in khaki regimental dress. They were obviously the commanding officers. One a cat and one a rat, they both cut impressive figures.

'Good evening,' the tall cat began in a broad Scots accent. **'WELCOME TO**

GLENVIEW CORRECTIONAL CAMP FOR NAUGHTY ANIMALS. My name is General Munro. You've all been sent here by your owners or the animal courts for being the naughtiest animals in the country.'

'He's got that right,' Toto heard Harry the Meowsider laugh under his breath.

'Some of you have been sentenced to a week here, others six months, but rest assured all animals will, if they play by the rules, come out of here well-adjusted members of animal society. However, if you don't play by the rules ...'

At that, the cat stepped back and his rat companion stepped forward with an even sterner look on his face and continued, 'Then I promise you a world of pain you will not want to endure. My name is Drummond, and this week will involve **THREE TASKS** you must complete as teams. The first of these will be explained tomorrow. If you want to go home, you have to pass the tasks. Dinner will now be served in the mess tent. We hope you *enjoy* it. Sergeant Major Gordon, over to you.'

The two officers disappeared back into their hut and Gordon barked, 'When you fall out, make your way to your tents; the numbers are posted on the notice board. Dinner is over in thirty minutes' time, and breakfast will be served immediately after our 5 a.m. roll call.'

'Ouch,' whispered Silver. 'Bang goes my catnap.'

'FALL OUT!'

The whole camp scattered, the new recruits running to the notice board as quickly as possible to see where they were billeted and bagsy the best beds.

'I say, you don't suppose they'll have

comfy beds and **FLUFFY PILLOWS,** maybe a
hot-water bottle, do you? And cocoa. I must
have cocoa before bed,' said Catface as they
followed the crowd. 'Also, I do like to insist
on my own bathroom. Do you think that will
be possible?'

'Catface, my old mate, I very much doubt it.' Socks frowned.

Sure enough, there were **DRAUGHTY TENTS, LEAKY TENTS AND HOLEY TENTS.** Tent number twenty-three was all of those things, and that was the one Toto and her friends found themselves in. In truth it should hardly have been called a tent; it was just moth-eaten canvas over a metal frame, with a wooden door.

'Well, I've stayed at the Ritz, but never the Pitz!' laughed Catface.

They left their belongings on the beds and made their way back to the mess hall for dinner. Sergeant Major Gordon bumped into them as they crossed the parade ground. 'I do hope you are enjoying our hospitality,' he growled menacingly. 'Nothing is too good for the budgie-hater of Croydon and her friends. I hope all our tasks are to your liking this week.' With that, he walked off whistling to himself.

'Blimey, sis, Larry could have given you an easier cover story. This guy's really got it in for you,' said Silver. 'So what's the plan?'

'I guess he's a big budgie fan!' answered Toto. 'Don't worry, it's nothing I can't handle. The plan? We'll wait for Larry's contact to reach out to me, but in the meantime the best way for us to see if Felis of Grampia does exist is to scour the local hills, lochs and so forth. For now, we **STICK TOGETHER** and take part in all the tasks, no matter how hard they are, but keep your eyes peeled for ways to get away from the rest of the crowd,

OK?' The gang murmured their agreement. 'Right, let's eat.'

'Woo hoo!' said Catface and Silver with a high-five.

Dinner was, as promised, VERY basic and not at all a 'woo hoo' affair: porridge. It was a cold stodge that, to Silver's horror, was made with water and salt. ('I've never heard of such a thing; not a drop of milk or cream in sight. It's inhumane, I tell you.') But he still ate it, and went back for seconds.

After such a long day, with full bellies and mindful of their early start, the cats all hit the sack and were fast asleep within minutes.

Toto stirred after a couple of hours. It was pitch black outside and all was still, but a slight movement at the foot of her bed had woken her.

Toto could sense a moving figure – the smell and the shape of the shadow she could just about make out suggested it was Catface. *He probably needs the toilet or, more likely, wants to see if he can steal some better food from the mess tent*, she thought.

'Catface, what's up?' Toto whispered, wiping the sleep from her eyes. The shadow loomed over her and immediately she could sense something was different about him. She turned to where Catface's bed was, and to her horror she could hear his snores. So, who was this? An attacker?

She sprang out of bed, spun the figure round and in a second had him pinned to the floor.

'What in Nessie's name are you doing?' he hissed in a loud whisper. 'Retract your claws, **RETRACT YOUR CLAWS!** You've gone and crushed my hat!'

The stranger was a rat who looked almost identical to Catface, dressed in a waxed jacket and flat cap. Toto could now tell he was neither a threat nor a danger, but who was he?

'The name,' he said, almost reading her mind, 'is Sandy Campbell, master poacher, head of food and beverages for Glenview Correctional Camp ... and Scottish attaché for one Larry the Ninja Cat.'

'So you're my contact! Sorry. But what are you doing sneaking around?' she asked, picking him off the ground.

'I didn't want to blow your cover. And I'm a poacher, so sneaking around is what I do. Plus there's strange goings-on in this camp. I can't quite put my forefoot on it, but the animals here don't appear to be getting any better at all. In fact, you could say **THEY ARE GETTING NAUGHTIER BY THE DAY!** It's not safe out at night so I like to keep my wits about me. All very odd. Now, let me fill you in on the wildcat – follow me.'

As they opened the tent door, moonlight lit up the rat and Toto could make out his shape. 'I know I can only see your outline, but you do seem to look an awful lot like Catface,' Toto said.

'I should think so ... he's my cousin!' answered Sandy. 'But I won't wake him to say hello now. Best let him sleep or he'll disturb the whole camp with singing, shouting and roaring. Plus he'll eat me out of house and home.'

'Hmm, I see you really do know him!' said Toto with a chuckle.

Sandy's wooden cabin was on the edge of the camp. A couple of times the pair had to jump into a nearby bush to hide from a patrolling terrier, but they made it without getting spotted. Sandy opened the door to a **ROARING PEAT FIRE** with two armchairs in front of it. To the left was a small table and a kitchen where, bubbling away on the hob, there was a saucepan of Toto's favourite: cheesy pasta.

'Larry told me you might be needing that, when the alternative is porridge, porridge and more porridge!' he said, mimicking Sergeant Major Gordon. 'Get settled,' he added, steering Toto to a comfy armchair and fetching her a bowl of the cheesy pasta, 'and I'll bring you up to speed.'

Toto chowed down on the frankly incredible pasta. ('It's the added haggis! It's my secret ingredient,' Sandy explained. Toto didn't have a clue what haggis was, but it was delicious.) She listened intently to the rat as he told her the whole story. His encounter with Felis, and how over the past few days the **LEGENDARY WILDCAT** had been spotted by locals far and wide. On the tops of mountains, at the foot of waterfalls, on the banks of lochs. The wildcat's intentions might be unclear, but Felis was definitely back.

'But Larry doesn't think he's real,' Toto interjected between mouthfuls.

'Well, Larry is a great ninja, but he's not here, and I know he cares little for our superstitions. Trust me, Toto, I've seen this cat take on a dog and a man – a **HUMAN MAN,** Toto – and win. There's no way it's just some cat tourist or vigilante; the legend is as real as Nessie ... I'm serious, Toto.' He paused, unsure how to proceed. 'If a real wildcat appears, they would hold a legitimate claim to the animal crown of Scotland. All the wildcat would need to take power is an army, and where better to recruit one than right here at the camp? A ready-made battalion of naughty animals. We could be looking at an animal war – it would be terrible!'

Toto pondered what to do next. This could obviously be **A LOT MORE SERIOUS** than Larry had suspected, but she needed proof, and ideally to find Felis for herself.

'Look, I'm here for a week. I have to take part in these tasks and, to be honest, I know I'm going to have to keep an eye on my brothers and Catface; there's no way they'll stay out of trouble. My plan is to try and scout the country for Felis as far as possible, then report my findings to the boss. He'll know what to do.'

Toto licked her bowl of pasta clean, then the new allies shook paws and Sandy escorted Toto back to her quarters, agreeing to meet again the following night.

'Look out tomorrow, Toto,' Sandy whispered as they neared her tent. 'This camp is becoming more and more dangerous. It's not just Felis you need to be worried about, ninja or not. I can't quite place why, but there's something in the air that's unpredictable ...' He saw the concern on Toto's face and tried to reassure her. 'Ach, it's probably just the worry of Felis getting to me.' He waved his arm as if to dismiss his thoughts.

But as Toto entered the tent and quietly slid into bed, she WAS beginning to be more than a little worried. If Felis was back and intent on raising an army, even with her ninja skills there wouldn't be an awful lot she could do to prevent it!

CHAPTER 5

'Rise and shine, you 'orrible lot!' Sergeant Major Gordon yelled at the top of his voice, the sound echoing around the glen.

Bleary-eyed and bedraggled, the camp's occupants all mustered on the parade ground. There were hundreds of animals: some who had been there weeks were looking cocky and blasé, others who had arrived the same time as Toto and the gang were looking fearful and apprehensive.

'Welcome to what for many of you is your first day at Glenview. And what a marvellous day it is here in the Highlands.'

They all looked up at the darkening clouds above.

'We have a nice easy challenge ahead of you today. Many of you have done it before, but by now you know the rules of the camp: if you can't pass the test ...'

'YOU SHOULDN'T HAVE BEEN A PEST!' the majority of the camp replied wearily.

'Exactly! You don't pass the challenges, you don't get to go home. So what shall we start with this week? We wouldn't want to overburden our new additions, so how about a nice gentle stroll up the hill?'

'That doesn't sound too bad,' said Silver as the rest of the camp let out a collective groan.

'You have twelve hours to get to the summit of Ben Canis and back,' he announced, pointing to a snow-capped mountain behind them.

Silver gulped. 'Scrub that, I can barely see the top!'

'Any animal who doesn't make it stays at camp an extra day. Any animal who tries to escape will be severely punished and stays at camp an extra day. Any animal who feigns injury stays at camp an extra day.' The Sergeant Major smiled. 'A fine breakfast of porridge awaits you in the mess tent. You leave in thirty minutes. Oh, and one last thing: **WE ENCOURAGE TEAMWORK** here at Glenview. Terriers, if you would be so kind ... ?'

The Border terriers made their way through the parade ground with some heavy-looking rope and proceeded to tie the animals together by the legs, four to a team.

'Teamwork makes the dream work,' Sergeant Major Gordon chuckled to himself. 'We'll be dropping in on you throughout the day to see how you are progressing. Anyone found to be tampering with their rope will be – you guessed it – severely punished and ...'

'Stays at camp an extra day,' the more seasoned members of the camp echoed back to him with resignation.

'*CORRECT!*' The Sergeant Major grinned. 'Enjoy your stroll. We shall see you back here at 5 p.m. Fall out!'

The camp's occupants all started to move to the mess tent for breakfast. It looked almost comical, like a huge three-legged race with the animals staggering around, some tied to creatures they'd never met before. The bearded dragons were tied to a beagle and a parrot (who was making her displeasure **VERY** apparent), and were having a truly difficult time of it.

Fortunately for Toto and the gang they were a very convenient four to be tied together, although that didn't stop Silver sprinting towards the mess tent and dragging the other three behind him.

'Did you hear him, sis?' Socks said as they munched on their salty porridge in the mess tent. 'We have to pass this test to even begin to think about getting home. And did you see how many animals have been here for weeks? It's **NOT GOING TO BE A PIECE OF CAKE**, this.'

'Please don't mention cake, dear boy,' said

Catface, staring mournfully into his sloppy porridge.

'You're right,' answered Toto. 'The only way we get out of this is to work together and make sure we get up to that summit and back, while also keeping an eye out for Felis. So eat up and let's get moving.'

The little gang felt as if they'd been walking for ages before they even reached the foot of the mountain, but the weather had held off and so far they had made good progress. The mountain path narrowed and grew increasingly steep, and pretty soon their fellow teams started to drop out. The group passed others who were complaining bitterly.

'It's too much. Even the porridge is better than having to get to the top of this blooming mountain,' lamented one small pug, who was tied to a sausage dog and a pair of exhausted chihuahuas.

Toto could tell that her brothers and Catface were tiring too, but they never moaned. They stopped only to drink some water and dunk their heads underneath a small waterfall.

At last they began to see the outline of the summit close above them. 'Almost there, guys, and we're making great time!' Toto encouraged them.

It was eerily quiet – Toto couldn't hear anyone else around them, only the distant call of a bird of prey. She glanced up again at the summit, but this time, along with the snow-capped peak, she thought she could just about make out something else: the shape of another animal, silhouetted against the sun.

'Silver, look up there – I need your eyes!'

Her brother turned to look. 'Mamma mia! You're right, sis. Could it be Felis?'

'There's only one way to find out – let's get a move on!'

The gang doubled their efforts and marched as fast as they could. As they were nearing the final bend in the path an eerie mist

suddenly descended, and **THEY COULD HARDLY SEE THEIR PAWS IN FRONT OF THEIR FACES.**

'I swear, it was just here,' said
Silver as they reached the
top of the mountain –
a small flat peak
shrouded in
mist.

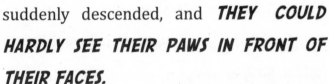

'Where do you mean? Over here?' said Catface, trying to be helpful. He rushed over to the far side of the plateau to look around, but in his haste lost his footing and slipped, tumbling over the edge of the mountain and dragging his three companions with him.

Tethered together by the rope, Socks and Silver hurtled behind him, over the edge. Toto was quickly being dragged off the mountain too. She reached out a claw, and just as she was about to follow her brothers into the abyss, dug it into the side of the mountain and clung on for dear life. **THE CLAW HELD, BUT ONLY JUST**.

Toto could feel the ropes around her ankles coming loose. 'Grab hold of each other!' she yelled. 'The ropes won't last much longer!'

She looked down and could make out shapes below, where her two brothers and Catface had managed to cling on to one another and were suspended in the air, and she could certainly hear their screams. All that was saving them from falling to their doom was Toto's single claw.

Even with her ninja strength and training she knew she couldn't hold on for too much longer. She felt around with her other paw for anything to grab on to, but there was nothing.

She slowed down her breathing, trying not to panic. She needed to conserve her energy and work out what to do. She knew she could hold on for a few more minutes, but after that ...

Maybe she could get Catface to climb up over the others and then help pull each of them up. She was still trying to come up with a plan when she heard a movement above.

'HELLO! HELP!' SHE CRIED OUT.

There was nothing but silence.

Then, just as all her hope was gone, a paw

suddenly appeared through the mist. She didn't know who it belonged to but she didn't care. With all her might, Toto launched her free paw and grabbed on tight. Surely there was no way whoever it was could support the weight of all four of them, was there?

Before she had time to process that thought, Toto was flying up through the air with her brothers and Catface in tow. **THEY LANDED IN A HEAP SAFELY ON THE PEAK OF THE MOUNTAIN.** As they looked around they saw a shadow disappearing through the rocks but in a moment it was gone, and with it the mist that had engulfed them all, leaving a clear sunny view for miles around. The four companions dusted themselves off and shared a reassuring – and relieved – hug.

'That was him, Felis. It had to be,' said Silver.

'Maybe,' replied Toto. 'Whoever it was, they were exceptionally strong and meant us no harm.'

'I thought we were goners then, sis,' said Socks, obviously not over the fright.

'Yes, huge apologies. I was *perhaps* a little hasty,' admitted Catface sheepishly.

'Don't worry, Catface, we're a team; mistakes happen. And whether that was Felis or not, they've gone now, so let's get back to camp before we fail this task.'

They all turned to head down the mountain, only to find their paths blocked.

'Going somewhere, are we?' Harry hissed, leaning up against a rock. **IT WAS THE MEOWSIDERS.**

'Oh, not again! Give it a rest, Harry,' said Socks. 'There's nothing to steal, no one to rob, we all have to get off this mountain, so do us all a favour and pipe down.'

'You little pipsqueak. I should have taught you more of a lesson on the train. Well, no one's around now. We're going to finish first in this task and you'll be lucky if you make it down in one piece. I'm gonna enjoy this. Gang, get them.'

Toto knew she couldn't break cover, but she could do the next best thing. She turned quickly to Catface and her brothers.

'Boys, remember your training and do what I say, when I say it ... OK?'

'You got it, sis,' smiled Silver.

They turned to face the Meowsiders.

As the gang surrounded them for what they thought would be an easy fight, Toto closed her eyes and let her whiskers and ears work out precisely where the bullies were. Certain of their position, she smiled to herself and began.

As the first gang member bore down on Silver, she waited for the exact moment, then whispered to her brother, 'Silver, sweep the legs.' He did exactly what he was told, and the yelping cat went down in agony.

Another whisper: 'Socks, tiger claw throw.'

One of the Burmese cats was sent flying into a heap.

And finally: 'Catface, round-house kick.'

The cat-rat connected with Harry's jaw with expert timing, sending **THE HUGE CAT SPINNING AROUND** and collapsing spark out.

The last cat looked on in terror, the fight

going out of her. She unsheathed her claws, cutting the rope that attached her to the other Meowsiders, and made off screaming down the mountain.

Toto slowly exhaled, then beamed with pride. 'You were listening in class!

Even you, Catface! Now, let's get down this
mountain. I'm not sure if that was Felis, but
one way or another we need to report it to
Larry. Plus I'm starving. Who fancies a nice
bowl of porridge?'

CHAPTER 6

The team arrived back in camp exhausted but happy. They had conquered the mountain and were the first group back. Sergeant Major Gordon gave them a begrudging nod as they traipsed back on to the parade ground. 'Not bad for a budgie-hater,' he growled at Toto, then turned to the other three. 'I heard you lot were a bit soft. Maybe I heard wrong.

Still, lots can go wrong in a week ... Get your beauty sleep; you'll need it tomorrow.'

With that, they were dismissed and stumbled back to their tent. They were so tired they forgot about dinner (porridge, obviously) and collapsed straight into their bunks.

As she drifted in and out of slumber, Toto could hear other groups of four returning in dribs and drabs. The last back were, much to Toto's amusement, the Meowsiders. She wondered what Sergeant Major Gordon would have to say, but to Toto's surprise it was General Drummond's voice she heard.

'What do you think you are doing?' the officer rat whispered furiously at them. 'You might not get another chance. If you want to make it and impress me, you'll have to do a lot better. Get back to your tents and don't fail me again.'

Toto was confused. What was the General talking about? Why did he care how the Meowsiders did in the task? Something very odd was up at this camp and Toto wondered if it could be connected to Felis. *Sandy might have an idea*, she thought to herself. And, as if by magic, right then the friendly rat appeared at the tent door.

'GOT ROOM FOR SOME SUPPER?' the poacher asked in hushed tones.

'You bet, cousin!' answered Catface as he, Silver and Socks bolted out of their beds, suddenly wide awake. 'I say, I don't suppose you have any of that cheesy pasta with haggis on top, do you?' Catface asked as they embraced.

'Aye, just as well I made a big pot. Come on then, and tread carefully or you'll wake half the camp up.'

'So do you think it was Felis we saw?' asked Toto after she'd explained the day's events, as the gang munched down on their supper in front of Sandy's fire.

'Without a clear sighting it's hard to say. But who else would have the strength to pull all four of you up? However, Larry won't believe it without proof. If it WAS Felis you saw, that's the second time he has helped a fellow animal. If I was raising an army, I'd want them to know I was to be trusted, and

///

what better way to do that than to save a couple of lives?'

'He's right, sis,' said Silver. 'Maybe we should try and contact him somehow to find out his plans. Although if he figures out

we've rumbled him, that might not be the best idea.'

'Well, we have to try, though I don't know how yet. And, Sandy, what about the Meowsiders and General Drummond?' Toto asked.

'Goodness knows what that is all about. Drummond and Munro only took charge a few months ago so maybe they are taking a more hands-on approach. I did say **THE CAMP IS GETTING STRANGER BY THE DAY.** Let's see how tomorrow's task goes, and keep your eyes out for Felis.'

'The leaky canoe is a legendary task here at Glenview. It requires nerve, teamwork, bravery and timing. And HOPEFULLY *doesn't* involve swimming.' Sergeant Major Gordon laughed.

It was a bright but very chilly morning and the camp residents were gathered on the shore of the icy loch. Still in their groups of four, each were stood in front of an old canoe that had obviously seen better days.

'Oh my eyes, looks like there's ice on the water and I'm still learning how to swim in the April Fools,' Socks said.

'What does that mean?' Silver asked Catface.

'I believe he said he's taking swimming lessons at a pool,' Catface answered.

'Ohhh, I know THAT. I'm taking him to the lessons,' said a confused Silver, shaking his head at his adopted brother's cockney slang.

'The task is very simple,' the Sergeant Major continued. 'Each team must work together to cross the loch, **BAILING OUT YOUR CANOE AS YOU GO.** We have put just the right number of holes in the canoes so that with enough bailing and paddling, you should be able to make it across without getting your precious tootsies wet. If not, you'll just have to swim for it.' He looked across the loch. 'It's only a mile away, and the water is freezing, so ... best of luck.' He chuckled to himself. 'On my whistle: three ... two ... one ... *Peep*!'

The whole camp ran forward and launched their leaky boats. It was a scene of utter carnage. In the rush to get their boats out on the water, some groups got trampled over by others, some got to their boats and immediately capsized, and some just didn't have the strength to start bailing out and **SANK IMMEDIATELY.** All the casualties made it safely back to shore, and within minutes only about a third of the boats remained on the open water heading for the far side of the loch.

Luckily Toto and the boys had got away safely and were setting a good pace.

Catface had made the rowing team at the University of Ratborough and had won several medals in the annual Animal Thames Games. 'Coxless fours, you know. I won gold three years on the bounce,' he said with a grin, clearly enjoying himself.

Toto and Catface concentrated on the rowing, while Silver and Socks were on bailing-out duty. For a while they made great progress, but just over halfway it became apparent that their canoe was leaking badly and they started to lag behind.

'I don't understand it, sis, we're bailing

out as fast as we can. We must have more holes than the others,' said Socks.

'Ahoy there! We HOLE-heartedly hope you get to the other side!' Harry and the other Meowsiders were falling about laughing in their canoe as they passed Toto's boat with ease.

'Blast, it was them.' Socks shook a paw at his enemy, who sneered back, 'Enjoy the swim, Socksie. Come on, guys, let's get a move on. Victory awaits!'

'Argh, sis, they're going to win!' Socks complained.

'We've got bigger worries than that,' Catface muttered. '*TOTO, THE BOAT IS SINKING TOO FAST. THERE'S NO WAY WE'LL GET TO THE OTHER SIDE. IS IT THE WRONG TIME TO SAY I'M A BIT SCARED?*'

'Me too, sis,' said Silver. 'This freezing Scottish loch is even worse than the Thames.'

'Don't panic, we're not finished yet,' Toto tried to reassure them, but the truth was, she was scared too. Touching her paw to the icy water, she could tell they wouldn't survive long if they capsized. No amount of ninja training could have prepared her for this.

She needed to get her bearings. 'How far do we still have to go?' she asked.

'Too far!' answered Socks with a sob.

'Yes, but we were aiming straight ahead to the far shore across the widest part of the loch. Is there anywhere else? Look around.'

'By Jove, what are the chances?' asked Catface. The rest of the party looked up in surprise. To their left was a tiny island, barely visible in the mist, only noticeable because a small fire had been lit on the shore. It was their only chance.

'Quickly, row with all your might!' Toto cried. All four animals gave up on bailing out and grabbed their oars. With Catface barking rowing instructions at them they rowed in perfect unison, never pausing until their paws and arms were burning. The tiny island got closer and closer, but as it did the water swilling around in the canoe started to rise, and with all the ice in the water the rowing became harder and harder.

'It's no use, Toto, we're stuck in the ice now!' screamed Silver. 'We're not going to make it!'

'Hang on,' said Toto. 'If we've hit solid ice, then maybe there's something solid enough to stand on.'

Slowly, Toto raised a paw over the gunwale

of the boat and tentatively put one hind leg on the ice. It creaked and groaned, but it held. She repeated the process and sure enough the ice was strong enough to stand on. **THEY WERE COLD, SOAKING AND STARVING, BUT WERE SAVED.** Stepping gingerly, they made it to the island and warmed themselves by the abandoned fire. When they had recovered a little, they made for the nearest shore, treading carefully across the ice, sticking to where it was thickest. Finally they safely made it to the bank and collapsed on the shingle.

'Congratulations!' said Sergeant Major Gordon sarcastically, appearing from behind a dune. 'Last place, but you still passed. You live to fight another day. Now only a five-mile hike home!'

Wearily the troop got to their feet and started to follow the Sergeant Major.

'You wait until I catch up with that Harry. He could have killed us,' Socks cursed.

Toto had no doubt he was right, but there was another thought that consumed her. **SOMEONE SOMEWHERE WAS HELPING THEM AND HAD PROBABLY SAVED THEIR LIVES TWICE.** Was it Felis? If not, who was it and why were they doing it?

The whole camp was asleep by the time the cats got back to Glenview.

'Bright and early tomorrow, when another wonderful challenge awaits. Sleep well!' Sergeant Gordon said mockingly as he left the four friends.

Her companions all passed out straight

away, but Toto crept straight to Sandy's cabin to fill him in on the mystery surrounding the burning fire and their brush with death.

'I have a hunch that Felis is keeping an eye on you for some reason. Toto, are you sure your friends didn't spot him at all today?'

She shook her head. 'No, just the fire. To be honest we were so tired and scared, we weren't really looking. We were just so grateful to be saved.'

'Hmm, well, I hear the task tomorrow will send you out into the wilds again, so if he wants to make contact, he'll find you.' They sat in thought for a second, but were interrupted by noises outside.

'Who the devil is that at this time?' Sandy went to tell the late-night prowlers to pipe down, but something in Toto's ninja training put her hackles up and she held her friend back. Putting a claw to her lips to tell him to be quiet, she silently moved closer to the window where she could listen to the conversation.

'It's Drummond and Munro. What are they doing skulking around the camp at this time?' Toto whispered.

'Well,' General Munro was saying, 'I think we have enough strength in the camp to make the march in the next few days.'

'Yes, it's all working perfectly,' General Drummond replied. 'It was a genius idea of yours to come here. The animals will undoubtedly be on our side, apart from those idiots Larry sent up and maybe that

budgie-hater bunking with them. It's a camp of the naughtiest animals in the country!'

'Yes, yes, but when we take over we need them to follow orders and be disciplined. And good at admin,' the cat replied.

'Of course.' The rat waved his companion's concerns away. 'There'll be time for all of that, but for now **WE NEED WARRIORS** who will destroy everything in their path!'

The two Generals were momentarily distracted by an unfortunate mouse who worked at the camp. She was passing by and tripped, dropping a tin of corned beef.

'Don't mind me – I was just heading to the toilet!' she squeaked as General Drummond picked the tiny rodent up by her tail.

'What did you hear?' the massive rat hissed. 'Not a thing I promise. Eek!'

'You know what, I believe you ... but why take chances?' And at that, the huge rodent smiled and threw the little mouse over the fence of the camp, where she tumbled down a steep bank into some painful brambles.

Toto and Sandy clutched each other's paws in disbelief, and it was clear even Munro was a little taken back by the rat's behaviour.

'I'm not entirely sure that was necessary,' said the cat.

'They have to learn, and they learn through fear; you never get anywhere with just respect. If we are to rule together, **ALL ANIMALS NEED TO FEAR US.** Anyone who questions us or stands in our way will be destroyed. So, see you tomorrow – eight-ish, OK?' he finished lightly.

'Err, OK ...' his companion answered uncertainly, then the two Generals went their separate ways.

'I don't think that whether Felis exists is our priority any more,' Toto whispered as the Generals' footsteps became more distant.

'I knew something was up around this camp! I told you the animals were getting naughtier and now I know why: these two have been raising an army in secret. You are right – this has gone way bigger than the legend of the wildcat. What should we do?'

'It's the work of an evil genius, all right: a ready-made army who will want to cause havoc. If the two most senior animals in the camp can't be trusted, goodness knows who else can be. *YOU'LL HAVE TO GET*

WORD TO LARRY personally. It'll be light in a few hours, so leave camp now and don't get spotted.'

'And what will you do?' the scared poacher asked Toto.

'You heard them. I'm still undercover, so for now I'll play along and compete in the next task. And at the same time I'll try and work out how to foil their plans.'

The cat and rat shook paws solemnly and parted. It was the most uncertain Toto had felt facing an enemy in a very long time. Stuck slap-bang in the middle of a restless army, **SHE AND HER BROTHERS WERE IN REAL DANGER.** She would have to tread very carefully.

CHAPTER 7

A miserable drizzle hung in the air as the camp assembled on the parade ground at dawn. Toto had filled her brothers and Catface in on the previous night's proceedings and suddenly the whole camp looked like a different place.

Toto figured that only the truly unruly and aggressive animals were being recruited to the army. The rest would be here for a week then shipped back to their owners. It must be why Drummond had recruited the Meowsiders to try and get rid of Catface and her brothers. Luckily, no one knew her real identity. For now, she was safe.

'Remember, every other camp mate could be an enemy, so **WE MUST TRUST NO ONE,**' she whispered to her brothers as they stood in the cold rain listening to Gordon announce the next task.

'For your final task this week, we have an oldie but a goodie. In your teams again, you must flee into the local countryside. In thirty minutes my colleagues here will track you down.' He gestured to the pack of Border terriers, who looked on menacingly. 'Avoid

them for three hours out there and you pass.
Pass this test: you get to go home. Fail: you
stay another week! On your marks: three ...
two ... one ... GO.'

**THE CAMP SCATTERED AND RAN FOR
THE HILLS, ALL WITH GENUINE FEAR ON
THEIR FACES.**

'They look nervous, sis,' Silver said,
looking around.

'With good reason,' added a weary Catface. 'Those terriers have a frightful reputation. I was talking to a mountain hare over breakfast; poor chap had his ear torn by one yesterday. Toto, my dear girl, we have to find somewhere to hide for three hours. I'm not sure I've got another long hike in me.'

'OK, let's get clear of the camp. I've got a place in mind.' She knew that Catface didn't have much left to give. The poor cat-rat was shattered (even his normally resplendent outfit looked a bit dog-eared) but she had to get as far away from the camp as possible before the terriers were let loose. She drove the gang hard and, cutting through the bracken, the sound of the camp became muted and distant. After a time, she heard a dull whistle sound and the dogs barking as they gave chase. Pretty soon after that they started to hear the yelps of the unfortunate creatures who were being rounded up. If they didn't get to their hiding place soon, they'd be caught and goodness knows what else.

Toto knew, too, that this task would be the perfect way for the Meowsiders to get rid of Socks, Silver and Catface. She needed to keep them all safe; perhaps the whole camp would be aware of their association with Larry by now, and if the Meowsiders tried to get them a third time, they might not be able to escape again.

She finally found what she was looking for: **AN OLD, ABANDONED BADGER SETT.** She had smelt it on their first hike up to the summit of Ben Canis as her sense of smell was so acute and, well, badgers were *so* smelly.

'You're not going to like this, but we all need to roll around in the earth, then get down the hole.'

'My dear girl, have you gone quite mad?' said Catface in horror.

'Yeah, sis, I'm not one to question you but it is a little pongy,' said Silver with his nose upturned.

'Exactly! If they can't **SMELL US,** they can't **FIND US.'**

The gang shrugged their shoulders in acceptance. Toto went first and the others grudgingly followed. Soon all four were covered in smelly dirt and safe, deep in the badger sett.

While Catface got some rest, Toto stood guard. So much had happened in the last twenty-four hours that her head was spinning and, even though she'd never say it out loud, she was unsure what to do next.

She'd come up here for what seemed like a relatively straightforward fact-finding mission and now she found herself in the middle of an animal army attempting a coup. And what of Felis; where did he come into all of this? She couldn't worry about that for now, all she could do was look after her brothers and Catface, then somehow try and delay the Generals until Sandy could get word to Larry for back-up.

Her thoughts were disturbed by rustling above and the familiar sound of a dog sniffing. Catface was fast asleep, but she gestured to her brothers to keep still as she listened intently.

For a second all seemed quiet, then slowly they heard the dog move away.

'Phew,' Socks whispered. 'Looks like that badger poo really has paid off—'

He was interrupted by the most **ENORMOUS SNORE** from Catface, which frankly could be heard a good half a mile away, let alone just outside the sett.

'Oh no, Catface, NO!' Silver hissed.

The call of 'Terriers! Alert!' was followed by frantic digging and snarling from above. The mouth of the tunnel was torn aside by three powerful, muscular dogs who entered the small sett and bore down on Toto and her comrades.

'GET THEM!' barked the leader.

The dogs bared their teeth and began to close in on Toto and the gang, forcing them into a corner. Toto was pretty sure she could take them, but they were ferocious fighters and given how tired Catface and her brothers were, she couldn't be sure they'd all make it out in one piece.

'Have to say, I'm gonna enjoy this. I've never liked cats or rats. Far too pleased with themselves,' one of the dogs snarled.

'In that case you won't appreciate this lesson very much.' A voice came from the entrance that made the dogs all turn towards it, straining their eyes. Its familiarity also made Toto freeze in her tracks. It was a voice she hadn't heard for a very long time. Then, suddenly, the owner of the voice flew out of the darkness, and with a series of **SWIFT KICKS** to one of the dogs' noses, knocked him out cold. Toto seized her chance and grabbed another of the dogs, throwing it over her shoulder so it collided with its fallen comrade and was knocked clean out. The third terrier looked at both Toto and the mystery attacker and didn't know where to turn. Its indecision was answered by two swift kicks delivered at exactly the same time by Toto and the newcomer. The poor mutt spun round seeing stars and collapsed on top of its friends.

WHO

The poor dogs must have been terribly confused. Why would their commanding officer, General Munro – dressed in his best army khakis – attack them when they were following his orders? For Toto too, confusion and fear coursed through her veins.

Munro stood up and dusted himself down calmly. 'Good afternoon, Toto.' 'Stone the crows,' mouthed Socks. 'That's—' **'ARCHDUKE FERDICAT,'** finished Toto. 'At your service,' her arch-enemy said with a bow.

CHAPTER 8

Toto could scarcely believe it. The last time she'd encountered her nemesis, he had escaped on a balloon from the top of the Holt Stage at the Catstonbury Music Festival. She'd often wondered where he'd ended up since then, but he was the last animal she expected to meet here.

'Get behind me NOW,' Toto commanded her

brothers and Catface. She took up her fighting pose, ready to face off with the Archduke.

'Calm down, Toto. As hard as this will be for you to understand, I come in peace.'

'PEACE? You don't know the meaning of the word,' scoffed Silver.

'That's hurtful,' replied ADF. 'I might have some issues with it, but I know its meaning. It means not fighting ... Doesn't it?' he asked, a little unsure.

'See! Get him, sis,' yelled Socks.

'Toto, before you and I engage in combat – which, I admit, would be **A LOT OF FUN,** I haven't had a good dust-up for ages – hear me out. Then, if you don't believe me and you **REALLY** want to, we can fight. And if you win, I promise you can take me back to

Larry and lock me up and throw away the key, blah blah blah. Deal?'

'I'm listening,' the ninja replied warily.

'Thank you,' he answered sarcastically as he sat down, leaning back casually on one of the passed-out dogs. 'Here, Socks, my dear young man, could you help me get these boots off? They're terribly uncomfortable.'

Incredibly, the little cat obliged; it was clear ADF was quite the charmer when he wanted to be.

NAAAR

'Oh, hello, Catface old chum. Nice to see you again,' he beamed. 'I say, do you remember the night back when Larry and I were at ninja school together and the three of us were so hungry we broke in and stole that whole fillet of beef from the Savoy ... Only naughty thing Larry has ever done! Wonderful night.'

'Wasn't it?' replied Catface. 'The most marvellous evening. I tell you what, the look on the chef's fa—'

'AHEM,' Toto interrupted, glaring at Catface.

'Ah, yes, sorry, well, you do know we were good friends once and he always has been *very* charming.'

The little ninja turned back to ADF. 'You are on the list of the world's most wanted animals, you have tried to kill me at least twice, you are the sworn enemy of my mentor, and you are currently in charge of an army about to march on Edinburgh destroying everything in its path. So **STOP CHARMING EVERYONE** and start explaining yourself!'

'All right, all right! Why does it all have to be so "business" with you goodies? You need to relax.'

Toto made to unsheathe her claws and ADF held his paws up in defeat – 'OK, you win!' – then crossed his legs and settled into his story:

'After you defeated King Roderick the Spotlessly Clean I tracked him down and enlisted his help. I needed a new army for my plans for world domination and since you sent my last two armies to prison, which was quite unsporting of you, I came up with a frankly ingenious plan. "Generals Drummond and Munro" would take over the correctional facility at Glenview and let the army come to US! All we needed to do was send the good animals back home, keep the really naughty ones here by making sure they failed their tasks, then get them onside and hey presto: you've got yourself an army of wrong'uns. *Ta da!*'

'Why are you telling us? Hasn't it worked?' Toto asked.

'It HAS worked ... too well. You might not have realised how big the camp has become, but we have over a THOUSAND animals who will do our bidding, Roderick has beefed up on an all-protein diet so he's in incredible shape, and **WE ARE MARCHING ON EDINBURGH TONIGHT.** Our plan is to take Edinburgh, then head south, conquering every city as we go, ending up in London, where we vanquish you and Larry, putting an end to the Ninja Cats, and I finally get to run the show. *Et voilà.'*

Toto was still confused ... **VERY CONFUSED.**

'He's up to something, sis. Get him,' Silver yelled.

'I'm not up to anything, my young Italian friend, so if it's all the same to you, can we leave the "get him" until you've heard me out. After all, I've saved all of your lives already, twice!'

'WHAT?' gasped Toto.

'Of course I have,' ADF said with glee. 'Who else did you think saved you? Up the mountain, who do you think pulled you all to safety? And who exactly do you think lit the fire that guided you to the island? *Moi!*'

'But we thought that was Felis,' Toto muttered to herself, now VERY uncertain what to think.

'Of course you did,' ADF continued. 'The legend of the wildcat has been VERY helpful to us. All of animal Scotland is talking about it, from Oban to Orkney. Only he doesn't exist. It's all an old fishwife's tale, and I assure you, I did once meet a fish's wife, Pippa, a pike. A bit bitey, but she told the tale very well. But it's been a wonderful distraction, allowing us to raise an army right under everyone's noses.'

'But the sightings?' Toto shook her head.

'Just some eager tourists and an old poacher with overactive imaginations.' ADF shrugged his shoulders.

'But hang on,' piped up Catface. 'Why the devil are you telling us all this?'

'Ah, the million-dollar question.' ADF smiled knowingly. As he did, one of the terriers began to come to, so the old ninja gave him a quick chop on the nose and he was out cold again.

'Where was I? Ah yes: it was all going to plan but I've hit rather a big snag. My problem, sadly, is Roderick. He's nuts! I simply can't control him.'

'But you're one of the finest criminal minds in the world,' said Catface.

'ONE OF? I am *THE* finest criminal mind. Look, you all know I want world domination, but I just want animals to run things since the humans are doing such a rubbish job. I don't want to have to kill anyone while doing it – I've never even wanted to kill Toto, really. I just want to take over Edinburgh and turn it into the envy of the animal world. I want the best secretaries, IT team, bin collectors, caterers, teachers, health care professionals ... You name it, I want to run it. Then everyone will believe in me, and I can be in charge of the whole world.'

The friends looked at each other, very confused.

'But Roderick wants to destroy EVERYTHING! It's tiresome and worrying. The other night he threw a little mouse over the fence into some nasty-looking brambles. The poor thing will be picking thorns out of her bottom for weeks. Well, you know me, I'm all about animal welfare, so that was the last straw. He's finally lost it. *I NEED TO GET RID OF HIM* and I need your help to do so.'

'What are you suggesting?' Toto asked.

'Well, tonight we are meeting at the top of the hill behind camp before we march on Edinburgh. There I intend to stage something of a coup, win over the mob, appeal to their better judgement and offer them all excellent, well-paid jobs in local government plus lovely families to be adopted by. You know the kind of thing: warm fires, cosy armchairs, treats on tap, etc. After all, what animal doesn't want to be loved? Most of this lot just haven't been cuddled enough. So when we get to Edinburgh I'll find homes for all the animals and I'll straighten up my act. Well, maybe not totally, but I won't be evil. I swear, Toto.'

'And what do you want from us?' Toto asked.

'Frankly, your muscle. There's a very good chance this will all go horribly wrong and even though I am an expert in combat, a beefed-up Roderick plus a thousand soldiers is beyond my capabilities. So you help me defeat Roderick, I disband the army ... then we can all go back to what we do best. You hunting me, and me thinking about non-violent ways of world domination. Deal?'

Toto's friends looked at her open-mouthed, unsure what she would do.

'If you betray me, I'll get revenge if it's the last thing I do,' she said, before sticking out her paw towards ADF to shake on it. **'DEAL. URGH. THIS FEELS SO WEIRD!'**

URGH

CHAPTER 9

'So what's our plan?' asked Toto as the unlikely allies huddled round for a pow-wow.

'Well, the thing that hasn't changed in all of this is how much Roderick hates you. Up to now, he hasn't seen through your disguise – which, by the way, is a *miracle* as it's just you dressed up as an old lady. But you know, he's not the brightest. I clocked you the minute you got to camp. So my idea is for you to show your true face when we are addressing the troops. He'll be so mad at seeing you he'll chase after you, leaving me to charm the army. Then we can round him up and work out what to do with him.'

'In other words, you want to use me for bait?' Toto observed.

'Weeellll, I wouldn't put it quite like that, but ... it's one way you COULD define the plan. What do you think?' he said with a grimace.

'I DON'T SEE THAT WE'VE GOT ANY OTHER CHOICE,' the ninja replied.

'And it's an excellent choice, Toto. You won't regret it,' ADF said as he put his boots back on. 'I'll see you at the top of the hill in three hours. I'll be on a small wooden stage at the front – wait for my signal to show yourself. I'll give you a subtle nod. Good luck.' With a trademark bow, he was gone.

'Sis,' piped up Silver, 'even if we do trust ADF – which I still have issues with – I'm really scared about this. Suppose we get caught?'

'I'm not crazy about it either, but **WE HAVE TO STOP THAT ARMY MARCHING TONIGHT.** Hopefully by now Sandy will have made contact with Larry and he'll be on his way with help. Until then, it's just us.'

By the time they left the badger sett, the sun had left the sky and they moved easily under the cover of darkness. As they got closer to the top of the hill, they could see the fires and torches where the crowd was gathering.

Toto turned to her brothers and Catface. 'You all stay here, safely out of sight. With any luck Roderick will give chase. I'll lead him a merry dance, let ADF work his magic and our job will be done.'

Silver put a paw on his sister's shoulder. 'Toto, I'm coming with you. With your eyesight, there's no way you'll be able to see ADF give his signal in the dark.'

'OK,' she agreed. 'But don't take any chances.'

'Good luck, guys!' Socks said nervously as his older siblings turned to make their way through the undergrowth to the clearing where the army were mustering.

A Border terrier guard patrolling the perimeter generously, if unwittingly, gave up its military beret and jacket for Silver to have an **ELEMENT OF DISGUISE**, as Toto swept its legs from underneath it with a kick and dragged it into the bushes. The cats then slowly melted into the crowd and cautiously made their way forward.

Roderick was on a stage built from old dead wood and bracken. His army were hanging on his every word.

'Tonight, my friends, we march into history to fulfil our destiny!'

'Oh blimey, not this old nonsense again,' Silver whispered to his sister.

'You have shown yourselves to be the naughtiest animals in the whole of Britain, and that loyalty to bad behaviour needs to be rewarded,' he laughed.

'Now that all the well-behaved goody-two-shoes animals have departed camp, I am left with the cream of the crop. **TONIGHT WE MARCH ON EDINBURGH, DESTROYING ANYTHING IN OUR PATHS!** From there we will march south, taking over every town. Any animal, be they pet or wild, who doesn't submit to our plans will be annihilated!'

'ADF was right; this guy is completely barmy,' said Silver.

The pair were now at the front of the crowd, and Silver could see that ADF had noticed their arrival. Ferdicat waited for a lull in Roderick's speech and gave an

exaggerated nod to Silver and Toto. But at the same time as Silver gave his sister the cue to reveal herself, Roderick noticed the strange behaviour of his partner in crime. 'Why are you nodding like that? You've put me off now! I was in full flow in my speech. Who are you nodding to?' He looked out into the crowd just as Toto removed her hat.

'Toto the Ninja Cat! You! How did I not see through that admittedly excellent disguise?'

'I don't think this is going exactly to plan,' Silver whispered to his sister.

Furious at the deception he had witnessed (and he was a pretty angry fellow at the best of times), Roderick was now yelling at ADF. 'I trusted you, and all this time you were plotting behind my back with her. Guards, seize them both!'

Silver suddenly grabbed his sister by the scruff of her neck, taking the initiative and pretending to be a guard. 'Don't worry, everyone, coming through. I've got her, don't panic, all under control.'

He couldn't keep up the pretence for long, as his disguise was so basic, but luckily it worked enough for them to get to the nearby undergrowth and dart for safety. As they did, Silver looked back to see the crowd move in on Ferdicat. Already the mighty warrior had bested fifty or so animals, but the numbers were too great and finally he was picked up and dragged away.

'Put him with the rest of the prisoners,

and when we take Edinburgh we'll put their heads on spikes!'

'Spikes! Yikes, let's get out of here, sis – we need a new plan.'

While the mob began their march – **BARKING, MEOWING AND SQUEALING WITH DELIGHT** – Silver and Toto ran as fast as they could back to the small clearing where Catface and Socks were waiting.

'I take it by the look on your faces that it did NOT go well?' Catface asked.

'Understatement,' said Toto. 'He's supposed to be a criminal genius so why did he make his nod so obvious?'

'I know!' Silver agreed. 'Mastermind, my paw! Still, can't be helped. We tried our hardest but best we get back to London, then Larry and the powers-that-be can sort this all out. Right, sis?'

'Sadly not, Silver. You're a ninja deputy now and we've sworn to uphold animal and human life, even if that life is an arch-enemy. You heard what Roderick said: **"HEADS ON SPIKES"**. And there are other prisoners too. We have to save them. But where will they be?'

'You're in luck there. While you were gone the prison guards passed by our hiding place, talking about heading back to Glenview. That's where they'll be.'

'Good work, Socks. Let's move. The whole camp will be heading the other way, so we should be able to get back without anyone seeing us.'

There was light coming from only one tent by the time they got to camp. It was obvious that ADF and the other prisoners were being held inside. Luckily, the guards weren't paying too much attention to anything outside, as they were so nervous about guarding the legendary Ferdicat.

Leaving her brothers, Toto was able to sneak up on the roof of a tent next door, then silently pick off the guards one by one. The dozy terriers didn't know what had hit them and within two minutes Toto had waved at her brothers to come and join her by the tent door.

Bursting in, they found ADF bound and gagged. As they untied him, he was hugely apologetic. 'Blast, I got too excited with my nod. I KNEW I should have underplayed it. Too eager; it's always been my problem,' he lamented. 'Well, I'm all out of ideas. What do we do now?'

'Toto!' Silver shouted. She turned to make out the shadowy shape of Sergeant Major Gordon tied up in the corner and next to him, to her horror, was Sandy.

'I'm sorry, Toto. They nabbed me as I was leaving camp to warn Larry,' Sandy said with a sob.

'But that means he has no idea about

what's going on, so help's not on the way!'
Silver gasped.

'And they nabbed ME when I found out
what was happening too. And they stole all
my porridge ... my poor porridge,' Sergeant
Major Gordon cried.

'Yeah, not quite as important,' said Silver.

'So, sis, there are seven of us versus, let's see …
A THOUSAND! Any ideas?'

'Sandy, how long will it take them to march
to Edinburgh?' Toto asked.

'They'll be there by nightfall tomorrow,
and even the quickest bird I know would take
a whole day to reach Larry with a message.
Ach, there's not enough time, Toto.'

The ninja thought quickly. 'Well, there's
only one thing to do. We'll send him a message
anyway, meet the army head-on in combat and
hope we can stall them long enough for Larry to
bring help.'

She turned to ADF and helped him up off
the floor. 'Shall we?'

'My dear girl,' he smiled. 'I thought you'd
never ask.'

CHAPTER 10

After Sandy dispatched a trusted hen harrier called Nigel down to London, the unlikely gang made their way across country to try and head off Roderick's army. Sandy and Gordon led the way.

'If we are to stand a chance, we have to get to Lowthers Pass before them,' said Sandy as they ran. 'That's the only way to get to the main trail to Edinburgh. It's a small gorge cut into the bottom of the mountain with sheer walls and a small river running next to it. It's so narrow you can only get out of it two by two, so it'll be a perfect place for us to stage an ambush.'

As they made their way there in haste, Silver noticed that **TOTO AND FERDICAT BOTH HAD HUGE SMILES** on their faces. 'Enjoying this, you two? On our way to almost certain doom?'

'Well, you can't say it's not exciting,' Toto shouted back. But her brother was right: all her life as a ninja, she'd been warned about the warrior she was now about to stand shoulder to shoulder with. It was an odd feeling and ADF seemed to sense her thoughts.

'Don't worry, little ninja. I feel it too, probably more so! I've been so fixated on defeating you and Larry, my judgement got clouded. But there's nothing like the heat of battle to make you see things clearly. Toto, it's an honour to be fighting alongside you.'

Toto smiled and nodded back.

'This is TOO weird,' shouted Silver.

'Sshh, we're approaching the pass,' Sandy whispered, calling them all to a halt.

They had made good time and, with an expert like Sandy leading the way, they had arrived before Roderick and the army.

Toto and ADF directed the rest of the team to take up positions on the hillside and before long they heard the march of a thousand animals coming their way.

'Remember,' hissed Toto, 'only reveal yourselves as they are coming out of the gorge on our side. On my call.'

'Gotcha,' said Silver, Socks and Catface in unison.

'Good luck,' whispered ADF. 'Remember: **PURRS, PAWS AND CLAWS.'** Toto couldn't believe he had uttered the Ninja Cat motto. 'Once a ninja, always a ninja,' he said, giving her a nudge.

By now the advancing army were directly underneath them in a bottleneck, just as Sandy had said they would be.

'READY IN THREE ... TWO ... ONE ... JUMP!'

The unlikely seven all landed exactly where they wanted, right in front of Roderick's army

RAAAAAAAR

at the mouth of the gorge. Roderick froze. 'You! You escaped! No matter. I've waited a long time for this. Ever since we fought on that viaduct, I've dreamt about this moment. And after I've dealt with her, I'm coming for YOU!' He pointed at ADF, then climbed up on to a nearby rock. 'Army: advance and destroy!'

Roderick's army slowly moved forward, but Sandy had planned their position perfectly; due to the narrowness of the gorge they could only get out into the open in twos. Which for two fully trained ninjas and five well-intentioned amateurs was a gift from heaven. Every time two animals exited the tunnel they were dealt with swiftly, Toto and ADF displaying their whole range of ninja moves. Almost showing off! Sweeping the legs, leaping over confused opponents and taking them out from behind, and they even once gave each other a high-five in mid-air as they bounced off the walls of the gorge and flew to deliver identical kicks.

Not to be outdone, Silver, Socks, Catface and Sandy were using an array of passable, if slightly clumsy, **HIGH KICKS, PUNCHES AND CHOPS** to good effect. Apart from once when Catface accidentally kicked Silver a glancing blow to the head. 'Sorry,' he winced.

EEK

Sandy was using some old poacher moves, popping in and out of the undergrowth

and delivering stealthy blows, then disappearing before he could be spotted. Even Sergeant Major Gordon was keeping up his end, having found an old saucepan and

using it to its full potential. 'This is for my porridge! You ungrateful so-and-sos!'

For a while it was going brilliantly but, sensing he was losing the battle, Roderick took drastic action. '*PUSH AS HARD AS YOU CAN,*' he shouted to his soldiers at the back of the gorge.

'You got it, boss,' shouted back Harry the Meowsider, who was marshalling the troops. 'You heard the boss. HEAVE!'

The army pushed with all their might to get through the tunnel. Toto and ADF did their very best to hold back the mob, but there were too many and finally the weight of numbers meant that the ninjas had to give way and Roderick's army flooded through the opening.

Toto, ADF and the others immediately stood back-to-back for safety as they were surrounded by Roderick's soldiers. For what felt like an eternity, the army held off, waiting for Roderick's orders as a slow mist began to gather around their paws.

'Brave, but ultimately your actions were futile. My revenge will be swift!' Roderick didn't seem to notice the **MIST CREEPING UP** around the waists of the animals, but his army certainly did and it was clear that they were uneasy. They began to turn to each other and murmur, 'It's a sign; no good can come from this.'

'IT IS NOT A SIGN!' Roderick screamed. 'It's just mist. You know, where water droplets are suspended in the air by temperature inversion and— This is NOT a science lesson ... I have no time for stupid superstitions so unless you want to join these traitors and have your head on a spike, I suggest you attack – NOW!'

But his army were no longer listening to Roderick. Instead, all eyes were firmly set above him in awe. Neither Roderick's army nor Toto's friends could believe what they were seeing.

An enormous cat stood almost motionless on a ledge overlooking the gorge. It was no ordinary cat, but a legend. **FELIS OF GRAMPIA HAD FINALLY SHOWN HIMSELF.**

'I knew it, I told you!' Sandy laughed with glee. 'No one believed me, none of you.'

Livid at the interruption to his orders, Roderick looked up to see what the

distraction was. 'But you can't be here; you're not real,' he said aghast. 'Destroy him!' he shrieked to his army. But it was to no avail. It was clear that all the animals who'd been loyal to Roderick had changed their allegiance to Felis. One by one they all knelt, which enraged Roderick even more.

'Fine, I'll deal with you myself.'

Roderick went to launch himself at the wildcat, but Felis was too quick for him. **THE WILDCAT LEAPT FROM THE LEDGE,**

WHOA

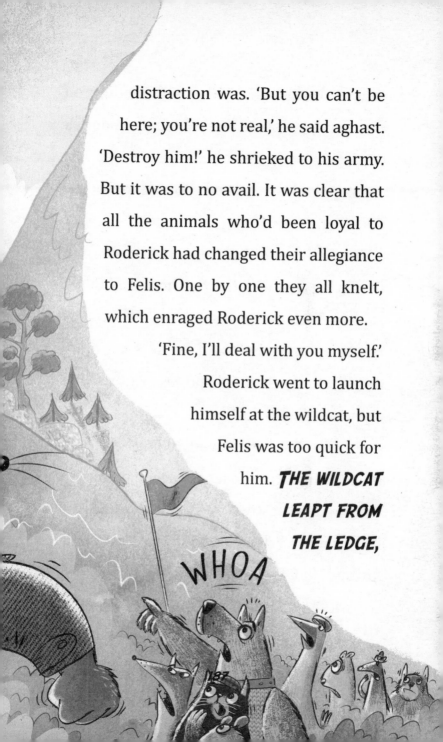

caught the rat in mid-air and, landing on the sandy ground below, sent Roderick sprawling by the river bed.

The wildcat turned to address the kneeling army.

'Yikes! It could be we've just gone from the frying pan into the fire here, sis,' Silver said to Toto under his breath. 'If this guy wants an army he could be an even more deadly enemy than old Spotless Pants. What are you going to do?'

But Toto's instincts were telling her not to do anything, and she let the scene unfold.

The giant cat stood on hind legs to address the crowd. 'Friends, thank you for your loyalty. My fellow wildcats appreciate it and we are thankful that you hold our names in such high regard. But we want no war; we don't want you to destroy anything. So go now with our blessing, back to your homes, your packs, your owners or make your way to your animal shelters where you'll be loved and cuddled. Go now and don't raise your claws in anger again.'

For a second the army didn't know quite what to do, but then slowly they began to get to their feet and talk in hushed tones. Toto heard several animals mutter to each other: 'I do actually quite fancy a cuddle,' and 'I can't wait to get back to the fire'. Even the Meowsiders trudged off.

'I don't believe my eyes,' said Catface. 'They are all going home, each and every one. Was that some kind of catcraft?'

There was one animal, though, who wasn't taking this lying down. 'You've ruined everything! That was MY army!' Roderick yelled.

A rock flew from the sandy bank of the river, jagged and rough, aimed straight for Felis's head. Sensing its direction, Toto launched herself through the air towards it. It was almost too late, but just as it was about to hit Felis square on the temple, the Ninja stretched her body as far as it could go and, deflecting the lethal rock with the very tip of her claw, sent it spinning through the air. Then, from nowhere a green flipper caught it before retreating back to the water, gathering up Roderick on the way.

He yelped, 'Something's got me ... Help me, please!'

But before anyone could go to his aid, the giant rat was pulled into the river. No one was quite sure what they were seeing as the mist on the water obscured the creature. ***IT COULDN'T BE ... COULD IT?*** They all stood in horrified awe, fully expecting Roderick to be dragged under to a watery grave. But then a quiet, gentle Scots accent piped up, 'What do you want doing with this one, Felis?'

'NESSIE? IT'S NESSIE AND SHE KNOWS FELIS!' Sandy flapped his paws in surprise. 'I need a lie-down and a nip of strong cream.'

'I think our guest might need some thinking time. I'd say six or so months with you on the remote Isle of Sásta with some anger management, yoga and maybe even tapestry will do the trick.'

YEEEEEEEOOOOW

WHOOOOO

'You've got it,' the giant reptile said with a laugh, before turning to swim away with Roderick screaming in her grip.

'No! Anything but tapestry! I'm terrible at it, I've no patience! *NOOOOOOOO!!!* I'll behave, I promise I will ...' His pleas grew fainter as the powerful reptile swam quickly downstream.

Slowly, they all turned back to Felis, who was still standing on the rock ledge.

'My king,' Sandy said, kneeling with a flourish. 'I would follow you anywhere.'

'Thank you, Sandy,' Felis smiled. 'But, like I said, my clan just want to be left to live quietly. And by the way, *IT'S QUEEN* – why does everyone think the legend must mean a king?'

'Eek! Sorry!' The rat shrugged his shoulders.

Felis turned to Toto, smiling. 'That rock was headed right for me. Thank you – you really are quite the warrior. I think the animals of the world will be safe enough with this little one at the helm.' She ruffled the ninja's head, then solemnly took off her hat and placed it gently on Toto.

Then, with a last nod, Felis leapt up the sheer face of the cliff in two bounds and disappeared into the dense bracken above. As she did, the mist around the gorge evaporated, leaving Toto and her party alone again, the only sound coming from the river rushing by.

Silver broke the silence. 'I'm not entirely sure how you are going to write this one up, sis?'

'Brother, I don't know where to start, and that's before I try to even begin explaining to Larry that our sworn enemy is now our trusted friend – right, Ferdicat?'

She turned to her old adversary, but where he had been seconds before, there was nothing but thin air ...

**JUST LIKE THE MIST,
ADF HAD VANISHED.**

EPILOGUE

Edinburgh's Waverley Station was abuzz with passengers and luggage as the animals rushed to make the departure of the Caledonian sleeper train that would take them back to London. Catface had insisted that they **TRAVEL IN STYLE** and had booked two berths for the four to share. Sandy and Sergeant Major Gordon (who had subsequently been promoted on the strict understanding that the camp didn't ONLY serve porridge and that rehabilitation through art, exercise, budgie appreciation and poetry should replace the old-fashioned tasks) had both come to see them off.

Sandy gave Toto an enormous hug and promised the ninja a lifetime's supply of smoked salmon: **'*JUST, NO QUESTIONS ASKED, OK?*'**

Silver and Catface were desperate to get to the dining car and were dragging Socks along, but Toto couldn't wait to be snuggled up in a real bed and get a good night's sleep. She was making her bed up as the train got ready to depart but something her whiskers prickle. She looked out of the window at the train opposite. She could only see the blurry shadows of the carriages so she pulled down the window to allow her senses to explore more. **WAS SHE IN DANGER?** She didn't think so, but there was a smell of something very familiar. The little ninja smiled as she realised who she had recognised.

'It's the aftershave, isn't it? My own fault; vanity getting in the way again. Catnip and sandalwood – I'll never learn,' Ferdicat said, smiling, as he hung out of the doorway of the train opposite.

'Why did you disappear? We owe you a great deal – if you haven't helped us **EDINBURGH WOULD BE OVERRUN**

right now, and Roderick would be in charge. As would you!'

'Urgh, I know, don't remind me,' he said, recoiling. 'Trust me, it's very odd, doing the right thing. I feel a trifle ill! I could have done a great job of running this town. I'd have made sure the trains were running on time for a start.'

'So what now?' she asked him. 'I'm sure I can smooth things over with Larry. Come back with us; we need you.'

'My dear girl, you most certainly don't – you're well on the way to being twice the ninja Larry or I were. **BUT DO SEND THE STUBBORN OLD GOAT MY LOVE.** I'll look him up next time I'm in town. No, I think I'll head north for a while and see where the wind takes me. I do still want to take over the world, you know. I say, doesn't that make me a wanted animal?'

'Yes, but I think we'll give you a head start. Let's say twelve or so hours before I get back to London and report seeing you. Thank you, Ferdicat, for everything. You might be a criminal mastermind but you stood up to be counted when it mattered.'

ADF looked touched and embarrassed. He doffed his hat to the little ninja gently and then, with a **SWISH OF HIS CAPE**, he was gone, leaving only the steam of the train in his wake.

Toto looked up and down the platform but her senses picked up nothing.

Smiling to herself she shut the window

and made her way to the dining car to find her friends. Maybe she was a bit peckish after all.

THE END

DID YOU KNOW THAT THERE ARE FOUR OTHER TOTO ADVENTURES?

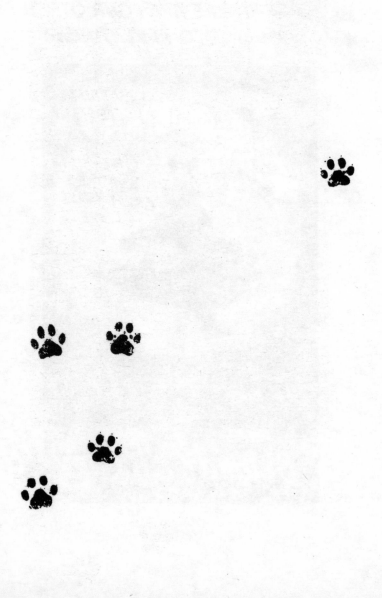

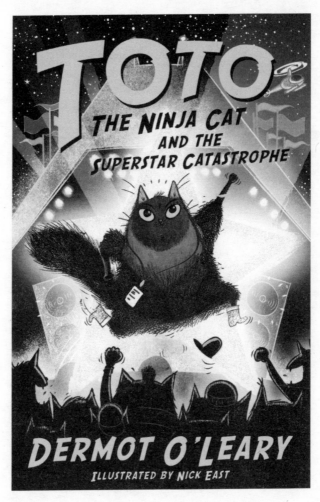

TOTO
THE NINJA CAT
AND THE
SUPERSTAR CATASTROPHE

DERMOT O'LEARY

ILLUSTRATED BY NICK EAST

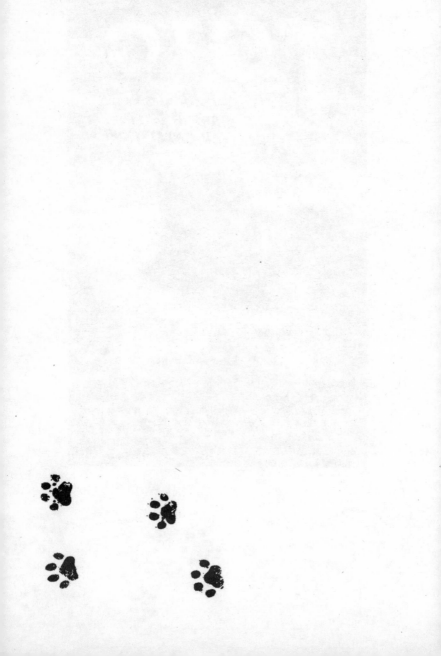

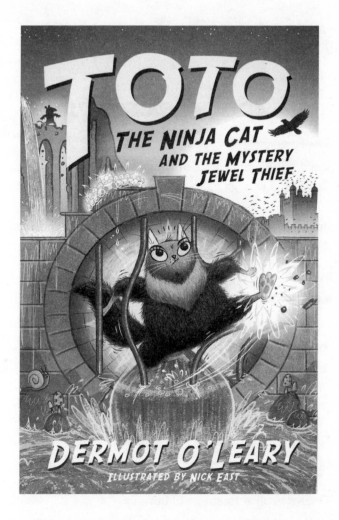

AND THEY'RE ALSO AVAILABLE AS AUDIO BOOKS,
READ BY DERMOT HIMSELF!

ACKNOWLEDGEMENTS

You'd think that lockdown would be the perfect time to write a book, and in many ways you'd be right ...

However, not being able to see people and do things really does make you realise how great people are. Go humans! And how much each and every Toto book is a team effort. It takes a village to raise a Toto. Now, if I could just find someone to type it for me, I could do three a year!

So, in no particular order:

To my brother in ink, Nick East. Thank you for bringing Toto and the gang to life. These stories wouldn't be the same without your talent, hard work, and passion.

Thanks to all at Hachette Children's.

The wisdom, grace, smarts and patience of Kate Agar.

The lightning in a bottle that is Alison Padley.

The dear departed Anne McNeil ... that was a trifle melodramatic – she's still with us in spirit if not in the office!

And the rest of the cat loving team ... at least they'd better be, if not they do an excellent job of faking it.

An honourable mention in dispatches to FL, who always goes above and beyond for team Toto, and is a proper champion of the independent book scene.

To the good people at John Noel Management: John, Jadeen, Darcey, Arqam, et al.

Thanks to team Toto and Socks at home. They really are spoilt, and don't deserve you. Sarah, Gosia, Fran.

To Kasper and Dee who always indulge my ideas, and provide an excellent distraction from getting any work done.

DERMOT O'LEARY'S

television and radio work, spanning over two decades, has made him a household name.

Dermot started his career on T4 for Channel 4 and has presented shows for both ITV, BBC, and internationally. His best-known work includes eleven series of 'The X Factor', The National Television Awards from 2010- 2019, 'Big Brother's Little Brother', UNICEF's Soccer Aid since 2010, the 2021 EE British Academy Film Awards alongside Edith Bowman and the 2017 Brit Awards which he presented with Emma Willis. Dermot is now a regular presenter on ITV's 'This Morning' on a Friday with Alison Hammond, and hosts BBC's Radio 2 Breakfast Show on a Saturday. His radio show is produced by Ora Et Labora, the production company Dermot co-founded in 2008.

Ora Et Labora also produce a number of podcasts including Dermot's 'People, Just People' podcast, launched with Audible in 2019 and now on its third series, that sees him interview a range of guests he greatly admires from the worlds of sport, fashion, politics and entertainment. It has featured interviews with Olivia Coleman, Arsène Wenger and Oti Mabuse. Dermot also hosts and co-produces 'Reel Stories', a BBC2 show looking back at iconic singers' lives on screen. He has interviewed legends such as Dave Grohl, Kylie Minogue, Noel Gallagher and Rod Stewart on the show.

In 2018, Dermot joined Kirsty Young and Huw Edwards to host the BBC's RTS Award winning coverage of the Royal Wedding in front of an audience of 13 million people.

Toto the Ninja Cat and the Legend of the Wildcat is Dermot's fifth children's book. He lives in London with his wife Dee, their son Kasper, and their cats Socks and, of course, Toto.